Poppyseed

Written by Stephen Cosgrove
Illustrated by Robin James

A Serendipity™ Book

PSS!
PRICE STERN SLOAN

The Serendipity™ Series was created by Stephen Cosgrove and Robin James.

Copyright © 1995, 1989 Price Stern Sloan, Inc.
Published by Price Stern Sloan, Inc.,
A member of The Putnam & Grosset Group, New York, New York.

Manufactured in China. Published simultaneously in Canada.
Library of Congress Catalog Card Number: 89-60560

ISBN 0-8431-3924-2

Serendipity™ and The Pink Dragon® are trademarks of Price Stern Sloan, Inc.

First Revised Edition
2003 Printing

Dedicated to Sharon Bukoskey, an aunt
of sorts, who brought me a cow that became
many cows, which nearly stole my heart away.

—*Stephen*

There have been many delights in the land of Serendipity. Trees have sung in the gently blowing mountain breezes. Clouds have slipped across the skies, warning of early spring storms that sometimes blew down into the valleys, all dressed in a mantle of snow.

The early spring snows would dust the meadows with a blanket of white, sometimes tickling the nose of a bunny that scampered about, leaving footprints for others to follow.

In this land of serendipitous delights was a quaint little farm. White board fences bordered this farm to hold some creatures in and others out. When winter finally slipped away, clover flowers and daisies popped up their heads beneath the snow as if to welcome spring.

In the barnyard ducks, geese, and old mother hens busily bustled about, arranging the food for spring and maybe a picnic or two when summer came. Here was a once mighty horse, still mighty with the pride of memory, but long past the age of plowing and pulling. He, too, felt the call of the springtime breezes with their tease of things to come.

But the best of the farm and of all who lived here were the cows that mooed in the meadow. Big brown eyes blinked in wonder at the springtime meadow. For what had been fields of snow the day before were now beginning to bloom.

They stood there, great heads lifted high above the fence, sniffing the air and breathing all the newness about them. Then one by one the cows marched to the meadow to taste firsthand the sweetness of spring.

Of this herd, there were three a bit more special than the others—more special because the mother, Merry Ellen, and the father, Tinker, had calved a late winter child. Late winter calves are rare, for normally all calves are born in the middle of spring. They named their calf after the winter poppy that grew, and because he was but a child, they simply called him Poppyseed, the beginning of new flowers to come.

Poppyseed had the best of everything, for being an only child in an adult herd can be a wondrous blessing. The bulls would butt with him in great mock battle. The cows would laugh at his antics as he chased a butterfly on his tail, around and around like a whirling dervish.

Whenever Poppyseed got into trouble, the others never scolded or punished him. One day he tried to eat the greener grass that grew on the other side of the fence. Unable to clamber between the rails, he tried to climb over the top. As is always the case in these kinds of situations, he did nothing more than get stuck.

Two of the bulls and three of the cows pulled and tugged him, and with a thump, he was on the same side once again.

But like all things, even the barnyard changes. With the warmth of spring and the promise of summer yet to come, the cows suddenly became edgy. Poppyseed had always been allowed to take lunch when he liked from any cow bearing milk, and this day he stopped, as he usually did, and began to sip a bit. But on this particular day, he was shooed away. Try though he might, none of the cows wished to share their milk. One of the cows, irritated by his insistence, even flapped him in the face with her tail!

Bawling, he ran about the meadow seeking his parents. "Oh, Mother," he cried, "the cows won't share their milk. Worst of all, they don't even want me around."

"There, there," mooed his mother. "It isn't you, my little Poppyseed, for this is the time of the others."

"Others?" asked Poppyseed, totally confused. "You mean to say that I am not the only one?"

"Yes," said his father, "during late spring the other babies will be calved, and then you will not be the only little one. You'll have brothers, sisters, and cousins galore."

And the others came. That day, and the next and the next, the meadow was filled with the sweet cries of newborn calves. Poppyseed looked on in wonder at this miracle of birth. One moment there was one very fat cow, and the next there were two cows—one a very tired momma and the other a wobbly legged newborn calf.

With the birth of the others came a great change in the meadow, and a greater change in Poppyseed's life. Before when he would spin around chasing butterflies on his tail, the herd would laugh at his antics; but now they paid him little mind. In fact they even called him a bother and told him to go away. It seemed that the little calves were more special. It seemed that they were all cuter than he was.

One of the cows told him that he was an older brother now, not a baby, and that he should make himself useful and help out, not goof around.

With the rebuff ringing in his ear and a tear in his eye, Poppyseed wandered from the herd, which didn't even notice that he had walked away.

It was then, in the confusion of his self pity, that Poppyseed decided to run away. He clambered upon the fence and though he was stuck for a time, no bull or cow came to his rescue.

"Silly cows!" he grumbled, as he picked himself out of the mud on the other side of the fence. "I don't need that old herd! I should become a horse and plow the fields—that will make me useful."

Trotting from the meadow to the old sun-bleached barn he found the harness and a plow. Once there, Poppyseed pulled and tugged on the harness and reins until, with a crash, they fell about his neck. With the gear tangled and wrapped about him, there was no way for him to walk, let alone pull a plow.

Luckily the old farm horse found him in the mess he had made. Laughing, the old horse pulled the gear off Poppyseed's back.

"Put that back!" cried the little calf. "If I am to become useful, I must carry the harness and learn to pull the plow."

"And why," asked the old horse, "would you ever want to pull a plow?"

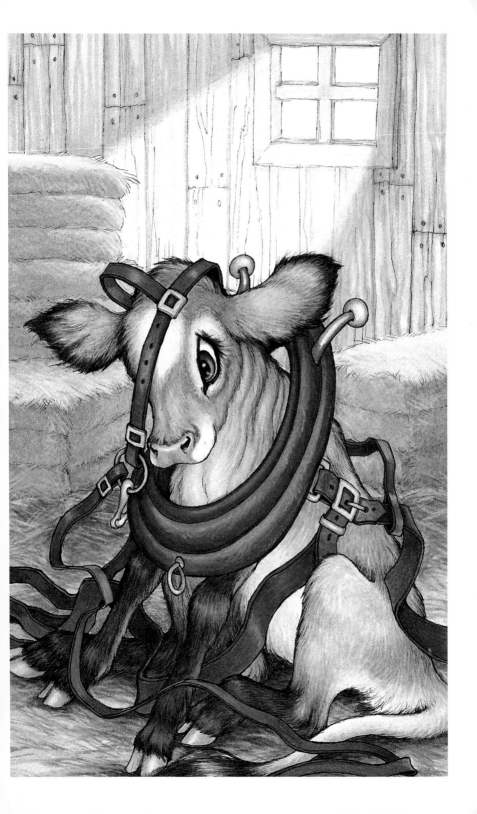

It was then that Poppyseed, with tears in his eyes, told the old horse the story of the calving in the meadow.

"Ah, little calf," consoled the old horse, "being a big brother isn't so bad. The little ones need to have bigger ones to look up to. They need to be shown what to eat and where to eat it and to be taught not to climb the fence. The little ones need an older brother to love."

All this made little sense to Poppyseed; he only felt unwanted in the barn by the horse. Sadly, with head held low, he went back over the fence and into the meadow. It was there that he bumped, quite innocently, into one of the little calves who was trying to eat a weed.

"Oh, don't eat that," Poppyseed sighed. "Weeds taste like dirt. Here, eat the clover and the grass; they are sweet to eat."

He patiently showed the little calf all the sweets to eat, and it wasn't long before he was surrounded by a small herd of little ones looking up to him in admiration. Unlike the older cows, the little calves didn't need to tell him to be useful, for he was. And more than that, Poppyseed was loved for what he was—an older, bigger brother.

IF INTO YOUR LIFE THE OTHERS COME,

BROUGHT TO LIFE BY YOUR FATHER AND MOTHER,

JUST REMEMBER THE CALF POPPYSEED,

AND HOW HE BECAME AN OLDER BROTHER.

Serendipity™ Books

Created by
Stephen Cosgrove and Robin James

Enjoy all the delightful books in the Serendipity™ Series:

Available wherever books are sold.

PRICE STERN SLOAN